Baby
Panda

SUSAN HELLARD

Piccadilly Press • London

Pu Lin and his mother lived together in a beautiful bamboo grove in the mountains of China.

When Pu Lin was a baby his mother carried him everywhere. She never put him down for more than a minute.

Pu Lin's mother found lots of crunchy
bamboo shoots for him to eat.
He grew bigger every day.

Pu Lin's mother was very proud of him.
"Now you are big enough to walk on your own
and to climb trees!" she said one day.

But naughty Pu Lin was rude to his mother.
"Walking is boring," he declared crossly.
"And I don't want to climb trees. Bamboo
shoots are boring, too! I'm tired of them."
He threw himself down and pounded the
ground with his paws.

"You are a sulky boy!" said his mother.
"I'll leave you on your own for a while
to think things over."
And she padded away to chew bamboo shoots
on the edge of the grove.

Pu Lin stomped off to the pool to have a drink. He lapped up the water till his tummy felt like a tight little drum.

Then he toppled over into the bushes.
"Everything is so boring," he groaned.

Suddenly, his mother sniffed the air. She smelled
danger. There were jackals nearby!

Silently and swiftly she ran back to Pu Lin.
"Hurry! We must climb up a tree to safety!"
she whispered. But Pu Lin was so full of water
that he could hardly move.

His mother grabbed him by the scruff of the neck and ran with him to the foot of a big tree.

"I can't carry you. You must climb
up yourself!" she panted.

"I can't! I can't!"
whimpered Pu Lin.
Then he looked round
and saw the jackals' eyes.

Pu Lin was so frightened!
Digging his claws into the tree trunk
he started to climb.

Higher and higher he and his mother
climbed – right to the very top of the tree,
far away from the jaws of the jackals.

Sitting at the top of the tree,
Pu Lin saw the most beautiful view.
Huge pine trees,
a great winding river,
distant snowy mountains,
and endless bamboo groves.
This wasn't boring. This was exciting!

Then Pu Lin found himself a little perch
where he could reach the highest,
juiciest bits of bamboo.
They tasted wonderful – not boring at all.

Pu Lin's mother called
to him. "The jackals
have gone. I can carry
you down now."
"It's boring being carried,"
said Pu Lin.
"I can climb down myself.
It's much more fun!
Come on, I'll race you!"
"That's my boy!" laughed
his mother.

Facts About Pandas

Pandas are found only in remote mountain areas of South West China.

Pandas have a gentle disposition and a slow, clumsy movement. Mature pandas are large and heavy. They have cat-like claws which make them agile tree-climbers, but they are awkward on the ground.

Pandas are almost exclusively vegetarian, with strong teeth for chewing fibrous vegetation – mainly bamboo. They spend all day eating.

Pandas seldom stray from the dense bamboo groves and clear mountain streams and rivers, although in summer they may move up the mountain to a higher altitude.

Pandas enjoy drinking almost as much as eating and are often reluctant to leave the river. They may drink so much their bellies become bloated and they can hardly move, making them flop down like drunkards.

Pandas do not hibernate or store food. They live alone and have no regular den, sleeping anywhere that takes their fancy, in clumps of bamboo or hollow trees.

Pandas may be attacked by a number of predators, including wolves, jackals, leopards or brown bears. They escape by climbing trees.

Females give birth after five months, usually to between one and three cubs. Only one receives its mother's personal care and the others rarely survive.

A baby panda weighs about 100 grams and is 13 to 15 centimetres long. It's born with closed eyes and has soft white down which develops grey then black patches over a few weeks.

Pandas can live for 25 years.
They are very playful,
especially after meals.